Rosalie
the Rapunzel
Fairy

To Harper Ribeiro, with love from the fairies

Special thanks to
Rachel Elliot

ORCHARD BOOKS

First published in Great Britain in 2016 by The Watts Publishing Group

A CIP catalogue record for this book is available from the British Library.

ISBN 978 1 40834 892 5

Printed and bound by CPI Group (UK) Ltd, Croydon, CR0 4YY

The paper and board used in this book are made from wood from responsible sources

Orchard Books
An imprint of Hachette Children's Group
Part of The Watts Publishing Group Limited
Carmelite House, 50 Victoria Embankment, London EC4Y 0DZ

An Hachette UK Company
www.hachette.co.uk
www.hachettechildrens.co.uk

Rosalie
the Rapunzel
Fairy

by Daisy Meadows

Join the Rainbow Magic Reading Challenge!

Read the story and collect your fairy points to climb the Reading Rainbow online. Turn to the back of the book for details!

This book is worth 5 points.

The Fairyland Palace

Fairyland Library

The Three Bears' Cottage

Island

Thumbelina's Cottage

Storybook World

Rapunzel's Tower

Red Riding Hood's Grandmother's House

Red Riding Hood Woods

Jack Frost's Ice Castle

Storytelling Festival Site

Wetherbury Village

Riverbank

Story Barge

Jack Frost's Spell

The fairies want stories to stay just the same.
But I've planned a funny and mischievous game.
I'll change all their tales without further ado,
By adding some tricks and a goblin or two!

The four magic stories will soon be improved
When everything soppy and sweet is removed.
Their daft happy endings are ruined and lost,
For no one's as clever as handsome Jack Frost!

Contents

Intruder in the Tower

"Hurry up, Kirsty," called Rachel Walker, skipping past colourful bunting and festival tents. "I can't wait to get to the Story Barge."

Her best friend, Kirsty Tate, had paused to look at a tent that was decorated with the first lines of lots of different children's books. She grinned at Rachel and ran to catch her up.

"That tent is amazing," she said. "I want to make sure I go back later and see how many first lines I recognise."

Rachel and Kirsty were having a wonderful weekend. Rachel was staying with Kirsty so that they could go to the Wetherbury Storytelling Festival together. One of their favourite authors, Alana

Yarn, was leading the festival and had arranged lots of fun storytelling activities.

"We did so much yesterday, it feels as if we've had a whole weekend already," said Rachel. "There was the *Goldilocks* puppet show and Alana's storytelling performance of *Thumbelina*."

"And we met the Storybook Fairies," Kirsty added, remembering the magical adventures they had shared with Elle the Thumbelina Fairy and Mariana the Goldilocks Fairy.

"And we've still got the whole of Sunday ahead of us," said Rachel, stopping to do a cartwheel. "I'm so excited! I wonder what Alana has planned for today."

"I hope we see the Storybook Fairies again," Kirsty added.

"I'm sure we will," said Rachel. "After
all, there are two magical objects still to
find."

The girls were secret friends of
Fairyland, but this was the first time that
they had met the Storybook Fairies. Elle
the Thumbelina Fairy had asked Rachel
and Kirsty to help them, because Jack
Frost had stolen their magical objects.
They had already helped Elle and
Mariana get their magical objects back,
but Rosalie the Rapunzel Fairy and
Ruth the Red Riding Hood's were still
missing.

The river was sparkling in the sunshine,
and as they got closer to the Story Barge,
the girls saw Alana Yarn standing on the
river path. When she saw them, she gave
a mysterious smile.

"This morning's activity is in a very special place," she said. "Go to the riverside playground and look for a tower. Then see if you can work out what this morning's story is all about!"

Kirsty and Rachel exchanged excited smiles. They waved to Alana and raced off along the river path to the playground.

"This is the best playground in Wetherbury," Kirsty told Rachel.

It was the biggest playground that
Rachel had ever seen. There were lots
of colourful swings, roundabouts and
seesaws, all surrounded by a bright
yellow fence. There were horses on
springs, climbing frames, tunnels and
even a speaking tube. In the centre of
the playground was a big slide, with a
tall, winding ladder that led to a tower
at the top.

"Do you think that's the tower Alana was taking about?" asked Kirsty.

"It must be," Rachel replied. "Come on, let's climb up and see what's at the top!"

They ran over to the ladder and climbed up. It was the tallest slide that they had ever climbed, and when they reached the top they found a small, round tower room with a small window.

Through the window they could see
across the park and down the river to
where the Story Barge was moored.
Some other children were already inside
the tower, sitting cross-legged on the
floor. Each of them was busy with a
sticker-activity book.

"Look, there's a pile of the activity
books in the corner," said Rachel.

The girls chose one
of the books and
sat down to
look through
it together. On
the cover was a
picture of a tall
tower with long,
blue hair coiling out
of the high tower window.

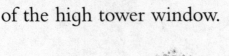

It was so long that it reached all the way to the ground, but the person who the hair belonged to was hidden inside the tower.

"It must be Rapunzel," said Kirsty, with a little shiver of excitement. "She's one of my favourite storybook characters."

"Mine too," said Rachel. "It's funny though – I didn't think that she had blue hair."

She opened the book and gasped at the picture on the first page. Someone was gazing out of the tower window, but it wasn't Rapunzel. It was someone with a spiky beard, a pointy nose and long blue hair. Rachel nudged Kirsty and showed her the page.

"Oh my goodness!" Kirsty exclaimed. "It's Jack Frost!"

Storybook Magic

Quickly, the girls flipped through the rest of the activity book.

"Every page shows a different picture of Jack Frost," Rachel said with a groan. "Where are all the pictures of Rapunzel that should be here?"

Kirsty checked the stickers in the book and looked up at Rachel with a worried expression.

"Even the stickers are pictures of Jack Frost," she said. "Look."

She held out the sticker page, where Jack Frost appeared in pose after pose, showing off his long blue hair.

"Why does no one else seem surprised by this?" Rachel wondered, looking around at the other children. "They're all just playing with the stickers."

"Let's ask them," said Kirsty, shuffling closer to a curly-haired little girl. "Excuse me, what do you think about all that blue hair?"

"Oh, it's beautiful, isn't it?" said the girl with a smile. "I wish I had long hair like that!"

"It's an amazing colour," added the boy next to her. "I might ask my mum if I can dye my hair."

"They haven't even noticed that it's not Rapunzel," Rachel whispered.

She and Kirsty felt worried and upset.

Jack Frost had ruined the Rapunzel story! The Storybook Fairies had explained that their magical objects gave the holder control of the stories. Of course, the fairies used their objects to make sure the stories went as they were supposed to, and ended well. But after stealing the objects, Jack Frost and his pesky goblins had actually gone *into* the stories and changed them. They wanted the stories to be all about them!

The other children were gazing down at their books again, but the girls didn't feel like looking at any more pictures of Jack Frost. Kirsty stood up and went over to the little window. She gazed down at the Story Barge, wishing that she knew how to return the activity books to normal. Then, out of the corner of her eye, she saw something moving. Rosalie the Rapunzel Fairy was fluttering outside the tower, waving to her!

Kirsty turned and beckoned to Rachel, then put her finger to her lips. The other children could not be allowed to spot the little fairy. Rachel came over and smiled when she saw Rosalie.

"Hello!" she whispered. "It's lovely to see you again!"

Rosalie waved to them and gave a gentle smile.

Her flowing purple
gown, sparkling
with teardrop-
shaped diamonds,
swirled around her
as she fluttered
outside the
tower. Her
long blonde
hair was
braided with
wildflowers,
and diamond
earrings dangled from her ears.

"Something terrible has happened," she
said. "Jack Frost has replaced Rapunzel
in her tower!"

"We know," said Kirsty, glancing back
at the activity books. "But no one apart

from us seems to have noticed."

"That's because Jack Frost has my magical hairbrush," said Rosalie. "He can make as many changes as he likes, and nobody will notice."

"But *we* noticed," said Rachel.

"That's because you are such good friends to all the fairies in Fairyland," Rosalie replied. "You even carry a little magical fairy dust in your lockets. You see things that other children might not. Please, will you help me to try to get my magical hairbrush back and fix the Rapunzel story? I don't think I can do it by myself."

"Of course we'll help," said Kirsty at once. "But what about the other children? We can't let them see you – or your magic!"

Rosalie peeped in through the tower window.

"They are all busy looking at their activity books," she said. "Besides, the storybook world is just like Fairyland. While you are there, not a single second will pass in the human world."

With a flourish of her wand, Rosalie made a tiny purple book appear in the air above her. It floated down to rest on her outstretched hand, and the girls saw the word "Rapunzel" on the cover in golden letters.

She opened the book and a breeze ruffled the pages.

Rachel reached out to take Kirsty's hand. Even though they had already been transported into two other stories, it still felt amazing to know that they were about to travel  into a book. Kirsty squeezed her hand and they shared a smile.

Rosalie tapped the tip of her wand on the open book, and some purple fairy dust sprinkled onto the pages.

Then she whispered,

"Storybook magic, please come to our aid.

Take us to where the stories are made.

Rapunzel needs help so we cannot delay.

We must stop Jack Frost and his goblins today!"

She took a deep breath and blew the fairy dust towards Rachel and Kirsty.

It swirled and twirled through the tower window, sprinkling the girls in tiny sparkles. They closed their eyes, and felt themselves being lifted up and whisked into the book.

A Long Climb

"What's that awful noise?" cried Rachel, clapping her hands over her ears.

She opened her eyes and saw that Kirsty and Rosalie also had their hands over their ears. They were next to a tower made of smooth, white stones. It was so high that a wisp of cloud was caught on the tip. There was a single window near the top, and someone was standing there, brushing their long blue hair.

"It's Jack Frost!" cried Kirsty, taking one hand away from her ear to point at the window. "Oh dear, I think he's trying to sing!"

It sounded like a hundred crows arguing with each other. Rosalie peered up at the window.

"I hope he's not using my magical hairbrush!" she said. "If it's in there with him, we will have to find a way to get it back."

Rachel walked around the tower. There was no door. All the way around, the wall was flat and solid. Trees surrounded the tower, and no one was in sight.

"There's only one way into this tower," Rachel said. "We'll have to fly up!"

"I can arrange that!" said Rosalie with a smile.

She waved her wand, and Rachel and Kirsty shrank to fairy size in a twinkling of fairy dust.

They fluttered their gauzy wings in
delight, hovering alongside Rosalie.
Together, they zoomed upwards. The
terrible singing got louder, and now they
could hear the words.

"I'm a genius, tra-la-la.

Goblins are idiots, tumpty-tum!

Stupid fairies, tra-la-la.

Clever me, tumpty-tum!"

"His singing is really hurting my
ears," said Rosalie. "We have to get him
to stop!"

But when they were about halfway up
the side of the tower, Jack Frost happened
to lean on his windowsill and look down.
He spotted the fairies straight away.

"What are you doing?" he yelled. "This
is my story now! You can't just fly up –
you have to ask me to let down my hair!

You're doing this all wrong! What's the matter with you?"

"We'll have to do what he wants, until we can get close enough to take back the hairbrush," said Kirsty.

She and Rachel looked at each other and nodded. They stopped flying upwards and hovered in mid-air. Then, together, they said:

"Jack Frost! Jack Frost! Let down your hair!"

The long blue hair
suddenly spilled out
of the window,
tumbling
towards the
fairies. They
dodged out
of the way
just in time,
but Jack
swung the
hair about like
a whip.

"He's trying to knock
us out of the air!" cried Rosalie.

She dived into the swinging blue hair
and clung on as tightly as she could.

"Hold on to his hair!" she shouted. "It'll
hide us from sight!"

Kirsty and Rosalie dived into the swishing hair beside her, and they hung on with all their strength. After a few more moments, the hair stopped moving, and the fairies heard Jack Frost cackle.

"Good riddance to bad fairy rubbish," he muttered. "I showed them who's boss! They don't dare to come near me now that I control the stories! Ha ha!"

Rachel, Kirsty and Rosalie exchanged grins and started to climb the hair. There was no way they could fly among the strands of hair.

They went as slowly and quietly as they could, pulling themselves up hand over hand. It seemed to take hours, but at last they reached the windowsill. One by one, they pulled themselves up and sat on the ledge, trying to catch their breath. Then they peered into the tower room.

Jack Frost was standing with his back to the window, gazing into a mirror on the wall. His blue hair was strangely lopsided.

"Why is his hair so wonky?" Kirsty asked.

"And why is there a piece of blue elastic under his chin?" Rachel went on.

Kirsty gasped. "It's a wig!"

As they watched, Jack Frost began to brush his hair again. The brush was blue with tiny golden flowers engraved

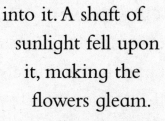

into it. A shaft of
sunlight fell upon
it, making the
flowers gleam.
"He *is* using
my magical
hairbrush,"
said Rosalie
in a whisper.
"We have to
get it back."

"But how?" asked Rachel. "The room
is empty apart from Jack Frost, and he's
holding the hairbrush. How are we going
to reach it without him seeing us?"

A Demanding Customer

Suddenly, Jack Frost whirled around and hurried over to the window.

"Come back into the room, blue hair," he said with a cackle. "You've done your work!"

There was no time for the three fairies to hide. He started to pull the hair into the room, and immediately spotted them sitting on the windowsill.

"What are you doing in here?" he screeched. "Spies! Sneaky little fairies!"

"Why are you wearing a wig?" asked Rachel, unable to control her curiosity.

Jack Frost glared at her so hard that his eyes seemed ready to pop out. His cheeks turned bright red.

"N-none of your business!" he stammered, clutching the magical hairbrush tightly. "Shut up! I'm not staying around here to be bothered by annoying little fairies! I'm going home."

There was a bolt of icy blue magic, and Jack Frost disappeared.

"Oh no you don't!" Rosalie exclaimed.
With a wave of her wand,
the three of them were
whisked upwards.
Words whirled
around them in the
air as they left the
storybook world
and were whisked
to Fairyland. Gasping
from the speed of the
journey, they found themselves fluttering
above the Ice Castle.

"Where did he go?" asked Rosalie.

"Listen!" said Kirsty, putting her finger
to her lips.

Echoing around the snowy hillside,
they could hear someone singing very
out of tune.

"I've got the hairbrush, tra-la-la.
The fairies are beaten, tumpty-tum!
They can't stop me, tra-la-la.
I'm so brilliant, tumpty-tum!"
"This way!" Rachel whispered.
She followed the sound of the singing
towards an open window in one of the
towers. Fluttering beside the window,
they peeped inside. Rachel and Kirsty
had seen Jack Frost's tower rooms before.
They were usually cold, grey and drab.
But this one was gleaming inside. It
looked like a hair salon, with glossy
surfaces, polished mirrors and rows of
curlers, combs and brushes. Bottles of
hairspray and gel lined the shelves.
Through an archway, the fairies could
see a supplies room packed with shampoo
bottles, hair bobbles, clips and pins.

Three goblins were working in the salon, each one dressed in a smart green uniform. While one of them was sweeping the floor, the other two were standing beside Jack Frost. He was sitting in a large chair and gazing into the mirror with a sad expression. Rosalie's magical hairbrush was still in his hand.

"I want long hair like Rapunzel's," he whined.

"We gave you long hair!" exclaimed a goblin hairdresser with a blond quiff.

He pointed to the blue wig, which was sitting on a mannequin's head in front of one of the mirrors. The blue hair was coiled neatly around the head.

"I want real hair of my very own, you fool!" Jack Frost shrieked, gripping the goblin by one pointy ear.

The other hairdresser, who had a large, fake moustache stuck to his upper lip, sucked in air through his teeth.

"Tricky," he said. "We can only work with what we've got, which isn't much."

"Would you like a fashionable fringe instead?" asked the goblin hairdresser who was sweeping the floor.

"You keep out of this," snapped the goblin with the moustache.

"Are you deaf?" Jack Frost shouted, shooing the quiffed hairdresser away. "I don't want a fringe. I want long, silky hair like Rapunzel's, and I want it *now*!"

Rachel gave a little quiver of excitement.

"I've got an idea," she said. "I think I know a way to get your magical hairbrush back, Rosalie. Follow me!"

She fluttered a little way around the tower to the window of the supplies room and slipped inside. When all three of them were standing among the bottles and hair accessories, Rachel turned to Rosalie.

"Can you turn us into goblin hairdressers?" she asked in a whisper.

Rosalie looked uneasy, but she waved her wand. Instantly Rachel and Kirsty's wings disappeared, their skin turned green and their faces grew mean and knobbly. They were wearing the same green uniforms as the goblin hairdressers, and Rachel had a mop of curly pink hair. Kirsty had a pointy orange beard.

They looked at each other and laughed.

"I hope I don't get the giggles when we're talking to Jack Frost," said Kirsty. "You look so funny, Rachel!"

"Please be careful," said Rosalie. "My fairy magic is not at its full power in the Ice Castle. It might wear off!"

"Then we will just have to be quick," said Rachel in a determined voice.

A Trick and a Trip

While Rosalie hid in the supplies room, Rachel and Kirsty strolled through the archway into the salon.

"Stand back!" Rachel cried in a haughty voice. "Make way! The best goblin hairdressers in the world are coming through!"

"Hey, this is our salon!" the goblin with the moustache complained.

"It's smaller than what we're used to," said Kirsty, sweeping past him to stand behind Jack Frost. "We will just have to make do! Now, Your Iciness, what sort of hairdo would you like?"

"We can do anything," Rachel added, putting her hand on his shoulder. "Long! Short! Crimped! Just say what you want and we will create it."

Jack Frost's eyes lit up.

"Really?" he asked. "Can you give me long hair like Rapunzel's?"

"No one can do that," said the goblin with the quiff. "I've tried!"

"But you are not the greatest goblin hairdressers in the world," said Kirsty, waggling a long, bony finger at him.

"We can make all your hairstyle dreams come true!" Rachel exclaimed. "But first I must brush out the tangles in your hair, so I will need to borrow your hairbrush."

She held out her hand, but Jack Frost frowned.

"I don't have tangles," he snapped, clutching the hairbrush to his chest.

Kirsty leaned over his shoulder and tugged at the front of his hair.

"It's full of tangles!" she said.

She was hoping to distract him so that she could grab the hairbrush, but Jack Frost leaped to his feet with a yell.

"You're not hairdressers," he yelled. "You're fairies!"

Rachel and Kirsty looked up at the mirror, horrified.
Their green skin was fading, and their long noses and big feet were shrinking. As they watched,  their wings appeared and their own hair replaced the wigs they had been wearing.

"Sneaky, tricksy, interfering fairy pests!" Jack Frost hollered, running around the salon. "You'll never get the hairbrush! Never, ever, *ever!*"

"Quick, Rachel!" cried Kirsty, grabbing the blue wig.

She threw one end of it to Rachel, just as Jack Frost charged towards the door into the castle corridor. They crouched down on either side of the door, each holding one end of the wig, and Jack Frost tripped over it as he dashed through the doorway. With a yell, he belly-flopped onto the floor and the hairbrush skidded away from him. Rachel sprang over him and seized the hairbrush.

"Rosalie!" she cried.
Rosalie zoomed
out of her hiding
place and took
the magical
hairbrush. She
beamed with
happiness as she
slipped it into her
pocket.

"I've got it back!" she cried in a
delighted voice. "I can't believe it!"

The three goblin hairdressers were
glaring at them with their arms folded
across their chests.

"I knew they weren't the best goblin
hairdressers in the world," said the goblin
with the moustache. "Neither of them
had a moustache."

"The best goblin hairdressers have quiffs, not moustaches!" squawked the quaffed goblin.

Squabbling, they disappeared into the supplies room. The three fairies looked at Jack Frost.

"It's not fair," he said with a sniff.

He was sitting up, but his head was bowed. As they watched, his bottom lip quivered. A tear dripped down his cheek and splashed onto the floor.

"I only wanted the magical hairbrush to get long hair like Rapunzel's," he mumbled.

He looked so unhappy that Rachel and Kirsty felt sorry for him. They kneeled beside him, took his hands and helped him up from the floor.

"My dreams never come true," he said

in a sad voice.

"You shouldn't have taken the hairbrush," said Kirsty. "You could have just asked Rosalie to help you."

"A fairy wouldn't help me," said Jack Frost.

Kirsty and Rachel looked at Rosalie. They knew how kind the fairies were, and they felt sure that Rosalie would want to make Jack Frost feel better.

Back to
the Tower

Rosalie's eyes twinkled, and she waved her wand. The blue wig rose up from the floor, shook itself out and then floated gently onto Jack Frost's head. Jack Frost patted his head. He wiggled it. He tugged on the hair. And then a wide smile spread across his face.

"It's real!" he cried. "It's really, really real!"

He ran to one of the salon mirrors and posed in front of it, practising flicking his hair over his shoulder and

twirling it up on top of his head.

"You goblins, get in here!" he hollered. "I want hairstyles! I want hair gel! I want bobbles and clips and slides! I want plaits and bunches and ponytails! Get to work!"

The goblin hairdressers scurried out of the supplies room, laden down with all the things that Jack Frost had demanded. Rachel, Kirsty and Rosalie looked at each other and laughed.

"Time for us to go, I think," said
Rosalie, pulling out her storybook.

When the pages
opened, the three
fairies were
whisked inside
the story once
more. Fairy
dust sparkled
around
them as they
arrived back
at the bottom of the tower. Rachel and
Kirsty were human again.

This time, they were not alone. A
dark-haired young man was standing
there, gazing up at the window. He was
wearing a velvet tunic with a golden belt,
and a cape swirled around his shoulders.

"It's the prince," said Rosalie in a delighted voice. "I think the story is getting back to normal."

"Rapunzel!" called the prince in a loving voice. "Rapunzel! Let down your hair!"

The girls waited, holding their breath. But there was no reply. Looking worried, the prince opened his mouth to call again, and then paused.

"Listen!" Rachel whispered.

Someone was singing in the tower. The exquisite voice rang out above them, and even the birds and butterflies flew closer to the tower to listen.

"Rapunzel is back," said Rosalie in a delighted voice.

The prince was smiling now, his eyes shining with love.

"Rapunzel!" he called again. "Rapunzel! Let down your hair!"

The girls looked up, and saw a young woman leaning over the windowsill. She smiled and waved when she saw the prince. Then her long, silky hair tumbled down from the window, and the prince began to climb up it. Rosalie turned to the girls and gave each of them a fluttery kiss.

"Thank you for helping me to get my magical hairbrush back," she said. "The story is unfolding just as it should, and it's all thanks to you."

"We're just relieved that Rapunzel and her prince are back," said Kirsty. "We've had a wonderful adventure."

"I will never forget your bravery and kindness," said Rosalie. "Goodbye – and thank you again!"

With a flourish of her wand, the tower,
trees and beautiful singing faded away.
Kirsty and Rachel were once more in
the playground tower. Around them, the
other children were still playing with
their sticker activity books. But now
there was no sign of Jack Frost and his
long blue hair. Every page and every
sticker showed a scene from the story of
Rapunzel, just as it should be.

"How is everyone
getting on?"
Alana asked,
clambering up
into the tower
room. Did you
all guess the
story before
you saw the
books?"

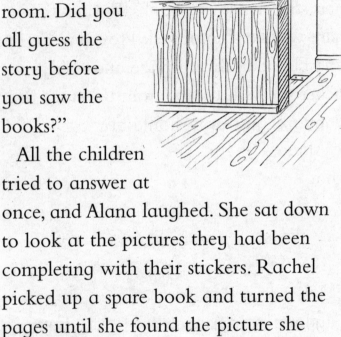

All the children
tried to answer at
once, and Alana laughed. She sat down
to look at the pictures they had been
completing with their stickers. Rachel
picked up a spare book and turned the
pages until she found the picture she
wanted.

"Let's colour in this scene," she said.

It was a picture of the prince reaching the tower window, having just climbed up Rapunzel's hair. The girls exchanged a happy glance and started choosing stickers.

"Alana, what happens after the prince climbs into the tower?" asked a boy.

"Rapunzel and the prince go off together to live in their own royal kingdom," said Alana. "It's a very happy ending – as all fairy tales should be!"

Kirsty and Rachel smiled at each other.

"I hope it's a happy ending for all the Storybook Fairies, said Kirsty. "We still have to help Ruth the Red Riding Hood Fairy to get her magical object back from Jack Frost and the goblins."

"We will," said Rachel, as she coloured in the prince's velvet tunic. "Like Alana said – all fairy tales have happy endings!"

Meet the Stroybook Fairies

Can Rachel and Kirsty help get their new fairy friends'
magical objects back from Jack Frost, before all
their favourite stories are ruined?

www.rainbowmagicbooks.co.uk

**Now it's time for Kirsty and
Rachel to help...**

Ruth the Red Riding Hood Fairy

Read on for a sneak peek...

"There's something so magical about a
campfire," said Kirsty Tate, warming her
hands as the flames flickered.

"I love staring into the flames," said her
best friend, Rachel Walker. "If you gaze
at them for long enough, you can start to
see pictures in there."

The girls leaned against each other,
feeling happy, sleepy and relaxed. They
had spent a wonderful weekend at the
Wetherbury Storytelling Festival, but
now it was Sunday evening and the fun
was nearly at an end. Together with the
other children from the festival, they

were sitting on logs in a circle around a campfire. Alana Yarn, one of their favourite authors, had helped to organise the weekend, and she was sitting on a log too. The girls had had a wonderful time getting to know her.

"So," said Alana, looking around the circle at them all. "Have you enjoyed the Storytelling Festival? What was the best bit?"

Everyone nodded and started to call out their favourite moments.

"The only bad thing about the whole weekend is that it has to end," said Rachel.

Alana smiled.

"We still have one more storytelling session before you have to go home," she said.

There was a large wicker basket in

front of her, and she began to rummage through it. Rachel turned and smiled at Kirsty.

"Thank you for inviting me to stay this weekend," she said. "It was a brilliant idea to come to the Storytelling Festival – I've had an amazing time."

"You're welcome," said Kirsty. "I'm really glad you came. I enjoy everything ten times more when you're here. It's been an extra-special weekend."

Read **Ruth the Red Riding Hood Fairy** to find out what adventures are in store for Kirsty and Rachel!

Calling all parents, carers and teachers!
The Rainbow Magic fairies are here to help
your child enter the magical world of reading.
Whatever reading stage they are at, there's
a Rainbow Magic book for everyone!
Here is Lydia the Reading Fairy's guide to
supporting your child's journey at all levels.

Starting Out

Our Rainbow Magic Beginner Readers are perfect for first-time readers who are just beginning to develop reading skills and confidence. Approved by teachers, they contain a full range of educational levelling, as well as lively full-colour illustrations.

Developing Readers

Rainbow Magic Early Readers contain longer stories and wider vocabulary for building stamina and growing confidence. These are adaptations of our most popular Rainbow Magic stories, specially developed for younger readers in conjunction with an Early Years reading consultant, with full-colour illustrations.

Going Solo

The Rainbow Magic chapter books – a mixture of series and one-off specials – contain accessible writing to encourage your child to venture into reading independently. These highly collectible and much-loved magical stories inspire a love of reading to last a lifetime.

www.rainbowmagicbooks.co.uk

"Rainbow Magic got my daughter reading chapter books. Great sparkly covers, cute fairies and traditional stories full of magic that she found impossible to put down" – Mother of Edie (6 years)

"Florence LOVES the Rainbow Magic books. She really enjoys reading now" Mother of Florence (6 years)

The Rainbow Magic Reading Challenge

Well done, fairy friend – you have completed the book!
This book was worth 5 points.

See how far you have climbed on the **Reading Rainbow**
on the Rainbow Magic website below.

The more books you read, the more points you will get,
and the closer you will be to becoming a Fairy Princess!

How to get your Reading Rainbow
1. Cut out the coin below
2. Go to the Rainbow Magic website
3. Download and print out your poster
4. Add your coin and climb up the Reading Rainbow!

There's all this and lots more at
www.rainbowmagicbooks.co.uk

You'll find activities, competitions, stories, a special
newsletter and complete profiles of all the
Rainbow Magic fairies. Find a fairy with your name!